This

treasure

belongs

to

No it doesn't.

It belongs to me . . .

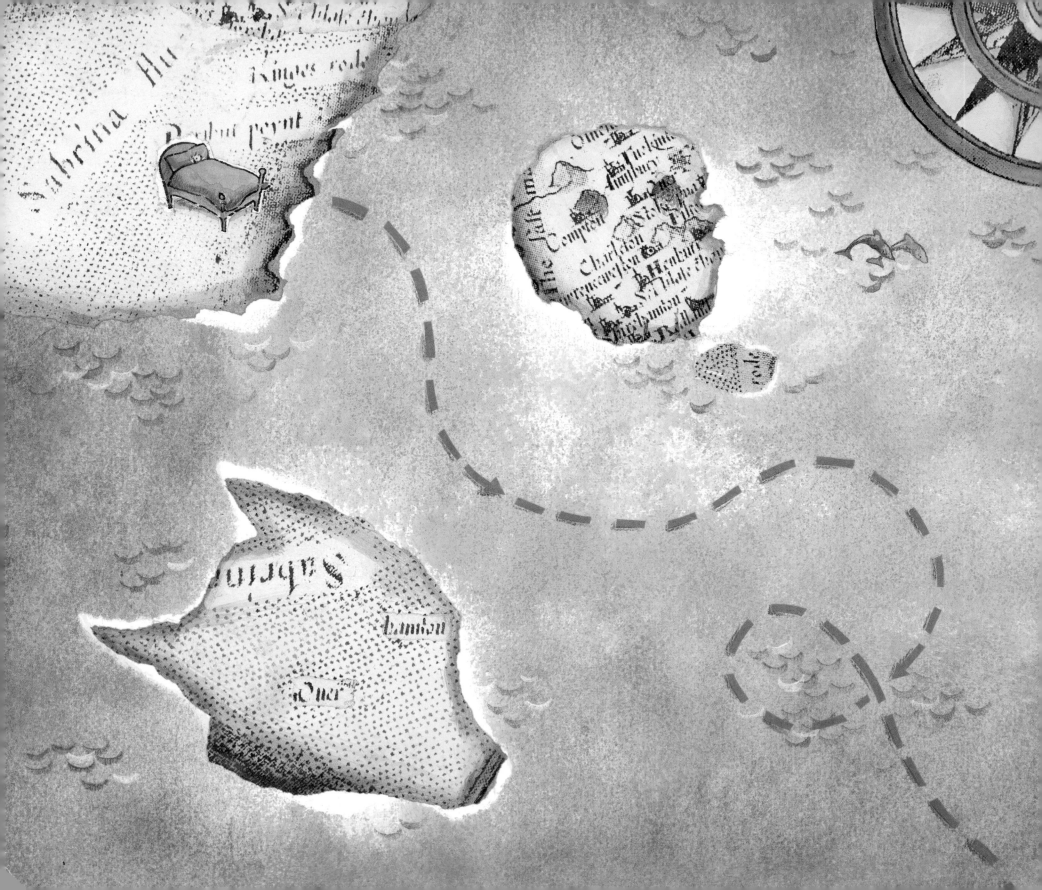

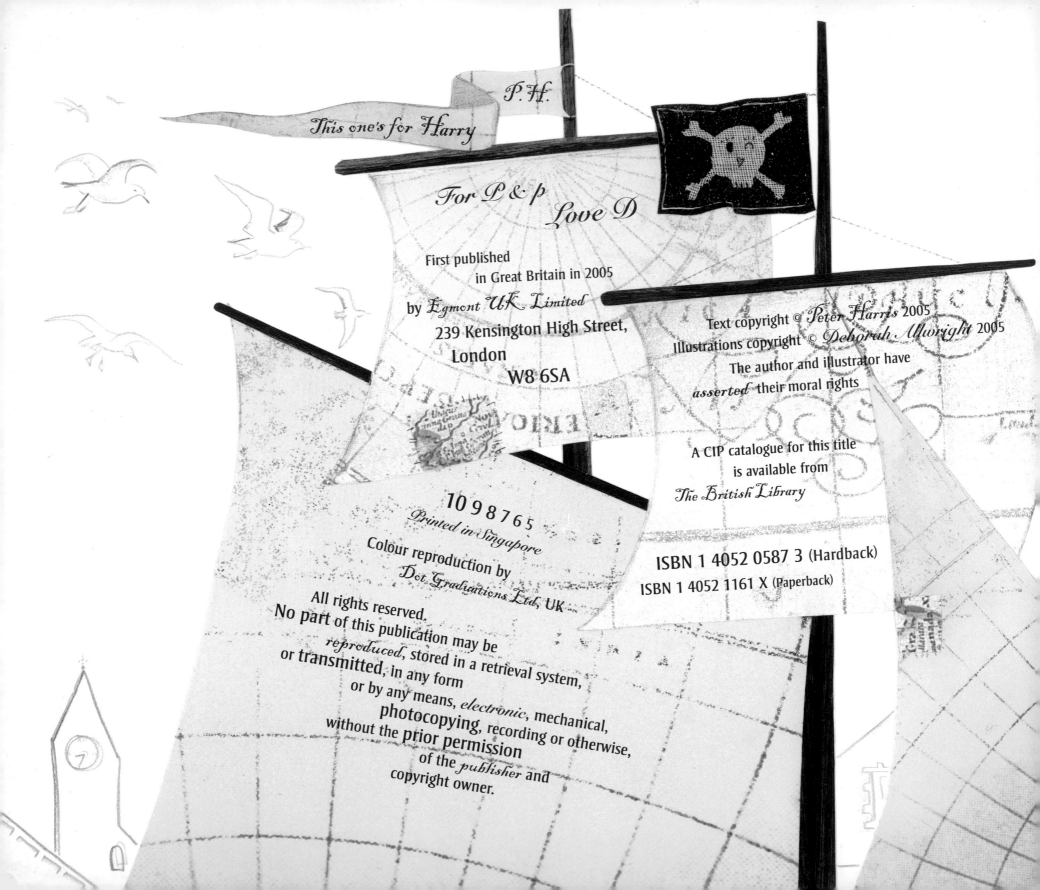

P.H.

This one's for Harry

For P & p Love D

First published
in Great Britain in 2005
by Egmont UK Limited
239 Kensington High Street,
London
W8 6SA

Text copyright © Peter Harris 2005
Illustrations copyright © Deborah Allwright 2005
The author and illustrator have
asserted their moral rights

A CIP catalogue for this title
is available from
The British Library

10 9 8 7 6 5
Printed in Singapore
Colour reproduction by
Dot Gradiations Ltd, UK

ISBN 1 4052 0587 3 (Hardback)
ISBN 1 4052 1161 X (Paperback)

THE NIGHT PIRATES

Peter Harris

Deborah Allwright

EGMONT

Down
down
down
the
dark
dark
street
they
came.

Quiet as mice,
stealthy as shadows.

Up

up

up

the

dark

dark

house

they

climbed.

Stealthy as
shadows,

quiet as mice.

Only the moon
was watching them
when they arrived.

Only the moon
was watching them
when they left.

Only the moon . . .

. . . and one little boy.

Tom was a nice little boy.
Tom was a brave little boy.
Tom was a little boy about to have **an adventure.**

Who were these shadows
as quiet as mice
stealing away with
the front of Tom's house?

**Maybe monsters
or trolls?**

**Maybe ogres
or gremlins?**

PIRATES!

Rough, tough little _girl pirates_.
With their own pirate ship.

A ship set for sailing.
A ship off on adventures.
A ship stealing the front
of Tom's house
for disguise!

But what about Tom?
Could he join the crew?

"**Please**

let me aboard!

Can I come too?"

And did the *girl captain* **say**,
"Certainly not!
You're only a boy!"

Oh no, not at all!
Instead she ro**ared**,

"Welcome aboard!"

Then **up** went the sails
and **up** went the flag.

Then off sailed the **rough,**
tough little *girl pirates*.

The little *girl pirates*
and their shipmate
Tom.

But where were they going?

To an island.

Where *Captain Patch*
and his **really rough,**
tough GROWN-UP pirates
were snoozing around their
full treasure chest.

Then *Captain Patch* saw **something**.

Something
very
strange.

Something very strange **indeed.**

What could he see?

A house
sailing
towards them,

getting closer
and closer.

A house sailing
towards them,
with a little boy
waving hello!

"I've seen a house!" *Captain Patch* declared.
"We've all seen houses," said the pirates. "Who cares?"

"Don't just lie there. **Do** something!" *Captain Patch* **roared**.
But the pirates went back to sleep and just **snored**,
while the house sailed nearer and nearer until . . .

. . . out
leapt
the
girl
pirates!

And out
leapt Tom!

And out leapt a fearsome **roar!**

The pirates gaped.

The pirates goggled.

Then the
pirates
all
r
a
n
a
w
a
y
!

So Tom
and the *girl pirates*
sailed away with
the treasure . . .

. . . while the
**rough, tough
GROWN-UP**
pirates
hid in
the
trees.

Captain Patch stamped his feet and shouted his **worst** pirate curse.

"If you don't give me my treasure back, I'll tell my MUM!"

But off they had sailed, all the way home.

Down
down
down
the
dark
dark
street
they
came.

Quiet as mice,

stealthy as shadows.

Up

up

up

the

dark

dark

house

they
climbed.

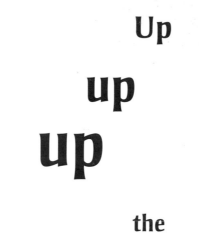

Stealthy as shadows,

quiet as mice.

Only the **moon**
was watching them
when they arrived.

Only the **moon**
was watching them
when they left.

Only the
moon . . .

. . . and one little boy.

Tom was a brave little boy.
Tom was a sleepy little boy.
Tom was a boy who had had an adventure.

And no one would ever find out . . .

. . . would they?

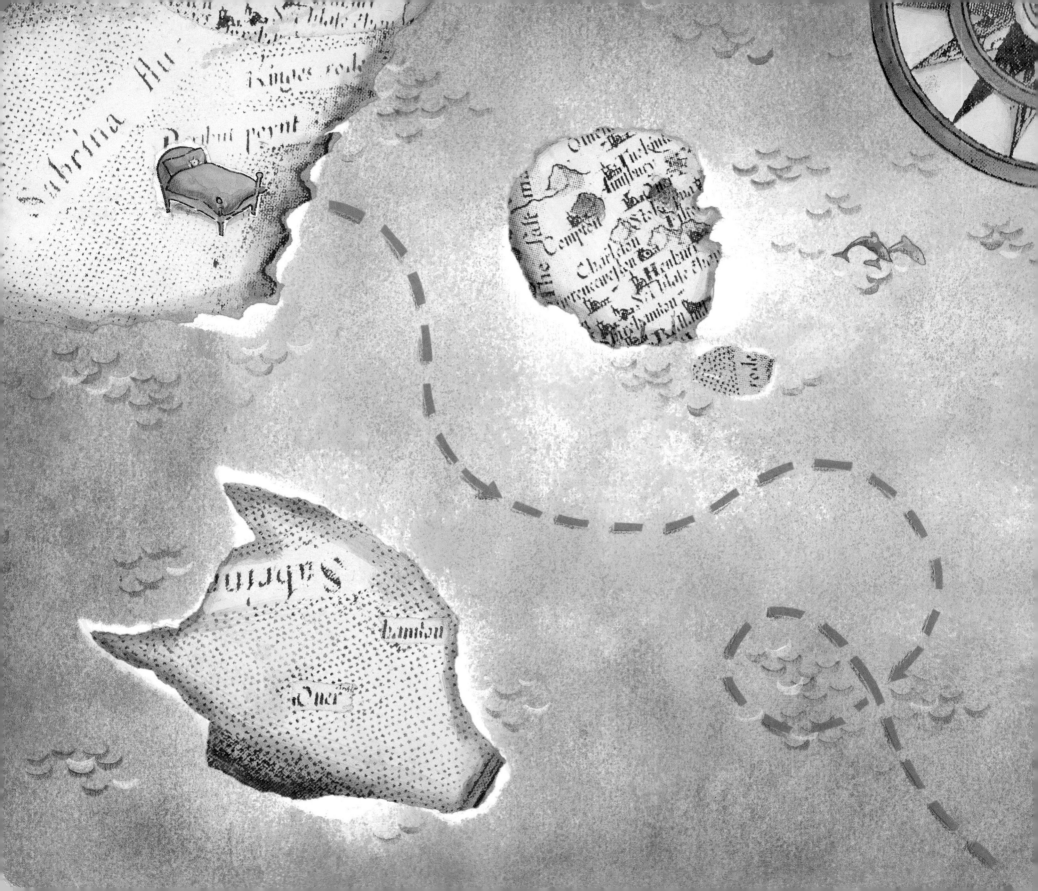